THE TREASURE DRAGONS

DRAGON GIRLS

Quinn the Jade Treasure Dragon

Maddy Mara

DRAGON GIRLS

Quinn the Jade Treasure Dragon

by Maddy Mara

Scholastic Inc.

Copyright © 2021 by Maddy Mara

Illustrations by Thais Damião, copyright © 2021 by Scholastic Inc. All rights reserved. Published by Scholastic Inc., *Publishers since 1920*. SCHOLASTIC and associated logos are trademarks and/or registered trademarks of Scholastic Inc.

The publisher does not have any control over and does not assume any responsibility for author or third-party websites or their content.

No part of this publication may be reproduced, stored in a retrieval system, or transmitted in any form or by any means, electronic, mechanical, photocopying, recording, or otherwise, without written permission of the publisher. For information regarding permission, write to Scholastic Inc., Attention: Permissions Department, 557 Broadway, New York, NY 10012.

This book is a work of fiction. Names, characters, places, and incidents are either the product of the author's imagination or are used fictitiously, and any resemblance to actual persons, living or dead, business establishments, events, or locales is entirely coincidental.

ISBN 978-1-338-68068-3

10 9 8 7 6 5 4 3 2 1   21 22 23 24 25

Printed in the U.S.A. 40

First printing 2021

Book design by Stephanie Yang

Quinn hummed to herself as she put her shiny golden trumpet back into its velvet-lined case. Around her, the other band kids chatted loudly as they packed up after practice. Everyone was excited. The big concert was tomorrow night!

Quinn was extra pleased because she had a

new tune in her head. Quinn loved writing her own songs. She looked around. She was too shy to play her own music in front of anyone else. But no one was paying attention. Maybe she could try it now?

Quickly, she pulled her trumpet back out of its case. She loved the smooth metal in her hands. It sometimes felt like her trumpet was a part of her. The loud part! Quinn began to play. The tune in her head flowed through the trumpet and out into the air. She repeated it, building on the melody as she went along. Quinn felt warm inside. It sounded even better than she'd hoped.

"That's beautiful, Quinn! What is it?"

Quinn spun around. Her band leader, Ms. Tran, smiled at her.

"It's not a real s-s-song," stammered Quinn. "I just made it up."

"Oh, it's definitely real," Ms. Tran said. "And it's great. Quinn, I'd like you to play it tomorrow, to kick off our concert. Would you do that for me?"

Quinn's hands went all sweaty. She loved playing in the school band. The way the different instruments all worked together felt like magic. They created something bigger and better than any of the musicians could create on their own. But playing a solo in front of everybody? She really didn't think she could do it.

But Ms. Tran looked so excited, it was hard to say no!

"Maybe," she said, fiddling with the jade-green bead in her friendship bracelet. She had made it with her jewelry-class friends, Mei and Aisha. They were both very brave. They wouldn't be scared about playing a solo.

Ms. Tran looked at her kindly. "You don't have to, Quinn. But it would be lovely to let others hear your music. Think about it and let me know tomorrow?"

"Okay." Quinn nodded as Ms. Tran strolled off, whistling Quinn's new song.

Quinn was about to return her trumpet to its case when she heard singing. It was familiar but very faint. Where was it coming from? She glanced around the room, which was now empty apart from Ms. Tran, who was stacking music stands.

Outside the window, Quinn saw the forest trees swaying. They seemed to be calling her. Quinn's heart began to beat faster. She was pretty sure she knew what was happening. Recently, she, Mei, and Aisha had discovered that they shared more than a love of making jewelry. They were also Treasure Dragon Girls! It was their job to protect the treasure in the Magic Forest. When they were needed, the ruler of the forest—the Tree Queen—called for them.

Quinn had a feeling this was happening right now! The words of the song grew clearer.

Magic Forest, Magic Forest, come explore…

Excitement swirled inside Quinn. She was definitely being called to the forest! She glanced down at her friendship bracelet. The jade bead at its center glowed bright green. As she watched, a warm, green light beamed out. The light whooshed around her and then shot into the mouthpiece of her trumpet.

Instantly, the trumpet turned an enchanting shade of green. Then the light beam flowed from the trumpet's bell, wider and brighter than before. The words of the song filled Quinn's ears.

Magic Forest, Magic Forest, come explore...

Quinn glanced over at Ms. Tran. Even though the music was getting louder, her teacher didn't seem to hear it. She was now busy arranging chairs.

Quinn gave her trumpet an affectionate pat. "I'll be back soon," she whispered. "But right now, the Magic Forest needs me."

Quinn looked at the beam of light. She could see trees inside it now! But these were not the bare, wintry trees like those outside the rehearsal room. These trees had the fresh, green look of spring. Quinn closed her eyes and breathed deeply as a warm breeze wafted past, heavy with the scent of mangoes, coconuts, and vanilla.

When she opened her eyes again, the beam

of light was big enough to step into. The song
filled her ears and she opened her mouth and
sang loud and true.

Magic Forest, Magic Forest, come explore.

Magic Forest, Magic Forest, hear my roar!

Taking a deep breath, Quinn stepped into the beam of light. The rehearsal room faded away. The green glow wrapped around Quinn, lifting her up into the air.

She was off on an adventure!

Quinn opened her eyes as she landed back on the ground. She was surrounded by trees dripping in shiny, ripe fruit. Vines curled around tree trunks, dotted with bright flowers. The ground was covered in mossy green grass, soft as velvet.

Quinn sighed happily. She had been to the Magic Forest a couple of times now, and it never stopped being exciting. In fact, it seemed more exciting every time! One of the best parts was turning into a dragon. In the real world, Quinn was often nervous. But when she was in the Magic Forest in her powerful dragon body, she felt like she could do anything.

Of course, when she was a Dragon Girl, Quinn couldn't play her trumpet. But that was a small price to pay for the joy of soaring above the treetops with her friends!

Quinn looked down at her shimmering green legs and paws. *And I can roar!* Quinn reminded herself.

To prove it, she let out a loud roar. Flickering jade-green flames leapt from her mouth,

and the air filled with a bright and wonderful sound. It just felt so good to roar. Quinn
laughed as she fluttered her elegant, powerful
wings, lifting gently off the ground. It felt good
to be able to fly, too!

One of the things Quinn loved about the
Magic Forest was how it sounded. It reminded

her of an orchestra. There were the low, rustling noises of the grasses and the reeds as the
breeze blew through them. Then there were
the chirrups of insects and the croaks of frogs.
Above this rose the melodies of the birds and
the whispering treetops. And around all that
swirled something that was more like a feeling
than an actual sound. It was a kind of happy,
humming feeling. Quinn wondered if this was
the energy of the forest itself.

But when the sound of Quinn's roar faded away,
she noticed the forest was almost silent. Quinn
couldn't hear any of the usual sounds. No frogs,
no insects, and definitely no birds. It was like the

forest soundtrack had been muted! All that was left was an annoying buzzing noise, like static.

"The forest sounds wrong, doesn't it?" said a voice nearby.

Quinn tilted her head to see a little bird hovering in the air. It looked a bit like an owl, but Quinn knew the animals in the magic forest were all different and utterly magical. The bird was green, and under each wing shone a brilliant flash of hot pink.

"I'm Flutterdash," twittered the little bird softly. "My voice is normally much louder, but the Shadow Sprites have been stealing all the forest sounds. So I'm losing my voice."

"That's terrible!" Quinn gasped. "Why are they doing that?"

The little bird flew even closer. "Without our sounds, the harmony of the forest is weakened," she explained in her tiny voice. "The bees can't hear the flowers calling to them. The birds can't listen for currents of warm air to lift them higher. The fish can't hear the warbling of the water, guiding them safely through the rivers. And that's only the beginning. It's a disaster!"

The little bird began to cough. Quinn had never heard a bird cough before!

"Better not talk anymore for now," said Quinn. She didn't want Flutterdash to lose her voice.

"Just nod or shake your head. Are you here to guide me to the glade?"

The bird fluttered her wings madly and nodded. Then she flew off, weaving her way between the trees. Quinn quickly launched herself into the air and followed. She didn't want to lose sight of Flutterdash.

Flying through the Magic Forest was strange

this time. It looked and smelled just the same, but it felt different somehow. Worse, the deeper Quinn flew into the forest, the louder the static sound became. Quinn could feel a headache brewing. Soon she could hear another sound: sharp, whispering voices. *You Dragon Girls won't beat us this time!* Right away she knew where that was coming from. The Shadow Sprites!

As Quinn flew under a low-hanging branch, something dropped onto her neck. Her throat began to feel weird and itchy. She shook herself, but the feeling stayed. Then she heard a sly voice, whispering right into her ear.

We have stolen most of the forest sounds already, the voice said. *Soon we'll steal your roar and the roar of your friends, too. Then the Shadow Queen will take over the entire Magic Forest!*

It took a lot to make Quinn angry. But this made her really mad!

Flutterdash flew up beside her. She didn't say a word, but Quinn could tell from her expression that she was worried.

Quinn felt a roar building up and a moment later, it blasted out of her, as loud as twenty trumpets playing at once. "There is no way you're getting my roar. Or my friends' roars!

And we'll get back the forest sounds. You just wait and see."

Instantly, the Shadow Sprite fell from her neck and turned to a gray dust.

"Don't worry," Quinn said to Flutterdash. "I seem quiet, but I can really roar when I need to! Now, how far are we from the glade?" Quinn hoped it wasn't too much farther. Dealing with Shadow Sprites was a lot better when she was with her friends.

By way of an answer, Flutterdash flew in a loop, then pointed up ahead with the tip of a wing. A warm, glowing light spilled through the trees. Quinn grinned happily. It was the glade, protected by its shimmering force field.

Quinn had been feeling tired after fighting off that Shadow Sprite, but seeing the glade filled her with energy. She couldn't wait to see the Tree Queen again. And her friends, of course!

As they reached the shining force field
that worked like a barrier around the glade,
Flutterdash paused.

"I guess you're not coming in with me, right?"
Quinn asked, hovering in midair.

The small bird nodded.

"Will I see you again?" Quinn asked.

Even though she and Flutterdash had only just met, Quinn felt that a special bond had already formed between them. Having Flutterdash flying by her side made Quinn feel stronger.

Again, Flutterdash nodded, her eyes bright. Then she darted away in a flash of pink and green.

Quinn turned to face the glade. The force field around it made a soft, special sound. Quinn had a feeling she was the only one who could hear it. She had always had sensitive hearing. She got it from her dad, who was a musician. The sound was a steady, comforting hum that seemed to vibrate in Quinn's chest.

As Quinn pushed through the barrier, she felt like she was taking a bath in pure music. Quinn closed her eyes, enjoying the feeling. She wanted to feel like this all the time!

"You're here!" cried two familiar voices once she was inside the glade.

Quinn opened her eyes to see her friends from jewelry class, Mei and Aisha. But they looked very different from how they looked in the normal world. They were both Dragon Girls, just like she was. Mei was ruby colored, with gorgeous gold and silver marking on the insides of her wings. Aisha's body gleamed blue, like she was covered in polished sapphires.

Her friends wrapped her up in a wing hug. "It's so good to see you," said Aisha. "Did you notice what's happening in the forest on your way here?"

Quinn nodded gravely. "Shadow Sprites are stealing the forest's sounds."

As she spoke, something rustled nearby. The Dragon Girls turned toward the magnificent tree growing in the center of the glade. Its branches swayed back and forth, as if blown by a breeze—even though the air in the glade was completely still.

Quinn's heart thumped. She knew what this meant. The Tree Queen was about to appear!

Sure enough, the tree began transforming into an elegant figure dressed in a flowing green gown. Her hair fell in dark waves around a kind and wise face. Her soft brown eyes twinkled as she greeted the group.

"Hello, Treasure Dragons," the Tree Queen said. "I'm so glad you're here. As you've already noticed, there is something terrible taking place in the Magic Forest. Our sounds are disappearing."

"How are the Shadow Sprites stealing the sounds, exactly?" asked Quinn.

The Tree Queen waved her branches. "That's a very good question, Quinn," she said. "It's all about the third object that the Shadow Sprites have stolen from the forest's treasure vault. As you know, they took the Forest Book and the Magic Mirror. You three have done a wonderful job of returning them to the vault. But one object is still missing."

Quinn thought about when she, Mei, and Aisha had been in the vault where the Magic Forest's treasure was kept. There was still one empty column, right in the center. "It's the Heartstring Violin, isn't it?" she said.

The Tree Queen nodded. "The Heartstring Violin is a precious and magical instrument. It is made from a branch of the Music Tree, one of the oldest trees of the Magic Forest. Its bow is made from the same wood. In fact, the Music Tree is an ancient ancestor of mine. A kind of great-great-grandmother. This violin is very old and very powerful."

Already Quinn was dying to hear this magical violin!

"What does it do?" asked Aisha.

"The violin makes music that guides all the sounds in the Magic Forest. Everything in the forest is in tune with it. The waterfalls, the whistling breezes, the barking of the foxes, and the squeaks of the mice. Without the violin's music as a guide, everything gets confused. And that confusion makes it easier for the Shadow Sprites to steal the sounds. The Shadow Queen has them locked away in her Ice Palace, up in the mountains."

"Well, it's not going to be easy anymore!" Mei declared fiercely. "The Treasure Dragon Girls are here!"

The Tree Queen laughed. "That's exactly

right," she said. "I am confident you will succeed, but I must warn you. This will be your most dangerous quest. Without the Heartstring Violin as a guide, many things in the forest are not working as they should. And the more time that passes, the stranger things will become. You must be ready for

anything. Rivers may flow the wrong way, for instance. And the animals may behave differently. You must be on your guard at all times. And you must guard your roars, too. They are your most powerful tool."

Quinn looked at her friends. She could see from their faces that they felt the same way she did. The idea of losing their roar was awful! There was no doubt the task ahead would be difficult. But Quinn was determined to return the violin to the vault.

"Quinn should be in charge this time," Aisha said. "She's the musical one."

Mei nodded vigorously. "And she seems to be able to hear things the rest of us hardly notice."

Quinn felt a little flush of pride. It was nice that her friends thought she should lead the quest. She only hoped she wouldn't let them down.

"I agree that Quinn is the right choice," said the Tree Queen. She bent one of her branches toward Quinn and dropped two objects at her front paws. Quinn recognized them instantly. The first object was the ancient compass that they had used on their previous quests. The second thing was the magical bag that Mei and Aisha had each worn on their quests.

When Mei wore it, it had turned ruby red to match her, and it was sapphire blue when Aisha had worn it. The moment Quinn put on the bag, a wave of brilliant green rippled across it. Quinn slipped the compass around her neck. She tingled all over with excitement!

She saw the Tree Queen looking at her intently. "Listen carefully, Quinn," she said, "and tell me what you can hear."

At first Quinn didn't know what the Tree Queen was talking about. But as she listened more closely, she realized she could hear something in the distance. "Is that a drum?" she asked. "It's very low and steady. It keeps going and going."

The Tree Queen nodded. "That's the heart-beat of the Magic Forest," she said. "Follow the sound. But you must hurry. As you can hear, the beat is very soft right now. If it stops, then I am afraid it will be too late to save the forest."

After watching the Tree Queen turn back into a tree, Quinn, Aisha, and Mei soared up into the air. It was time to get started on this quest!

4

As the Dragon Girls flew high above the Magic Forest, Quinn hummed a song. She didn't usually sing in front of others, but she needed something to fill the silence. Even the wind made no noise as it whipped by. Quinn found herself humming her new song, just to break the unnatural quiet.

"You've got a great voice, Quinn," Mei commented, flying alongside her.

"You really do," Aisha agreed, doing loops and twirls as she flew along. "Can you sing a song for us?"

Quinn was glad that it was impossible to know when a Dragon Girl was blushing. "I only like singing with others. Solos freak me out! But actually, I shouldn't be singing anyway. We are supposed to be listening for that drumbeat."

"Good point," Mei agreed. "Can you hear it?"

Quinn strained her ears. For a moment, she thought the beat had disappeared. She wished she hadn't been distracted by humming her song! That was the problem with music. When Quinn got a tune into her head, she forgot everything else.

But hang on ... there it was! A distant, slow drumming.

They had been flying high above the tree line. It was faster up there, without any obstacles in the way. But the beat was too faint up that high.

"We need to fly lower," Quinn decided.

"Lead the way!" Aisha called back cheerfully.

Quinn swooped lower. Soon, she and her friends were weaving through lush forest trees, which silently rustled their leaves.

"That drumming sound is changing," Quinn said.

"I can't hear anything," Mei said.

"Really?" said Quinn. To her, the drumbeat was building in volume. And now she could hear other sounds as well. It was like more musicians were joining in, adding to the original beat.

"I can't hear anything, either," said Aisha. "You must have amazing ears!"

"My ears are bright green and pointy," Quinn joked. "So I guess they are pretty amazing."

She was a big fan of her dragon ears. She loved the way they swiveled around so she could pick up sounds coming from different directions. She wished her human ears could do that!

Quinn spotted something up ahead through the trees. In a glow of colored light, some small shapes moved around. The drumming was definitely coming from there.

A moment later, the trees opened up and the Dragon Girls found themselves in a small clearing. Before them was a most surprising sight! The surrounding trees were decorated with garlands of bright flowers. Dotted around the edge were freshly dug holes. And in the center of the clearing, a group of small creatures danced in a circle. They had tiny eyes but very big paws, which they were stamping and clapping in complex rhythms as they hopped around.

Quinn and her friends landed in a huddle. "Are those badgers?" Aisha whispered.

"They look like it," said Mei. "But I thought badgers didn't really like coming aboveground."

"That's true for much of the year," piped up a little voice from nearby.

They looked down to see a tiny badger peering up at them. He was wearing an elegant

waistcoat made of purple velvet. His claws
sparkled like gold, and the white stripe that
ran down his nose was threaded with silver.

"But today is the annual Beat Fest," continued the badger. "All the Beat Badgers of the

Magic Forest come aboveground for the day.
We dance and sing together. We can't see very
well, but our hearing is wonderful."

Quinn tilted her head. The drumming was coming from the circle of dancing badgers. She knew most instruments, but she could not tell what was making this rhythm. "What kind of drum are you playing?" she asked.

The badger clapped his paws together excitedly. "It's not a drum at all," he said. "It's an old violin! We are drumming on its side to the rhythm of the forest beat."

"A violin?" said Quinn, a flash of excitement streaking through her. Surely this was the Heartstring Violin they were looking for! But her excitement was almost immediately replaced with alarm. "Why are you *drumming* on it? You might break it!"

The Beat Badger looked offended. "Badgers are very careful," he said, huffily adjusting his vest. "Anyway, the violin was already scratched. It has no bow or strings, either. But it makes a lovely sound when we drum our paws on its side."

Quinn glanced at her friends. Clearly they were all thinking the same thing: They had to get that violin back! Quinn approached the group of badgers. She walked softly, so as not to scare the little creatures. Unfortunately, it's not easy to be quiet when you're a huge and powerful dragon. The Beat Badgers soon heard her coming. Grunting in alarm, they scattered in all directions, leaping into their burrows heads first.

"Look!" Mei whispered, coming up beside her. "There it is."

In the middle of the clearing lay a violin made of a beautiful honey-colored wood. It was very old and scratched. Just as the Beat Badger had said, the violin had no strings. And there was no sign of the bow, either. But even though it wasn't in great condition, Quinn could tell that this was a powerful, precious instrument.

A part of her wanted to snatch up the violin and fly off with it. They could get it back into the vault, and all the wonderful forest sounds would soon return. But Quinn knew that it wasn't the right thing to do. She would be devastated if someone took off with her trumpet!

Quinn turned in a slow circle, looking at the ring of burrows. She was pretty sure the badgers were still close to the surface and would be able to hear her. "I'm sorry," she called out. "I didn't mean to scare you."

A badger in a mustard vest popped its head out of a tunnel. "Well, you did!" the badger said.

"It's not very nice to ruin our dance party like that," said another, wearing a jade-green vest that matched Quinn's scales.

"We've already had to move twice because of those pesky Shadow Sprites!" said yet another, peeking her head out of the ground.

"I can't believe they tried to steal the beats from the Beat Badgers," muttered the badger in green.

"We'll leave you alone," Quinn said. "But first I have a favor to ask. We need to take this violin with us. You see, this isn't a normal instrument. It's the magical Heartstring Violin. We need to get it back into the vault, where it belongs."

Several badgers popped up their heads.

"That's the Heartstring Violin?" exclaimed one. "It should NOT be out here!"

"That's why all the sounds are messed up in the forest," said another, clapping its paws to its face in shock.

"Exactly," said Quinn. "So is it okay if we take it? The Tree Queen has tasked us with returning it."

"Of course it is!" cried a number of badgers.

"Don't make a mountain out of a molehill, Dragon Girl. Clearly it needs to be returned." The badger in mustard velvet chuckled.

"But what about your dance party?" Aisha asked.

"Don't worry about us," said the badger in purple. "We're also great singers."

At that, all the badgers burst into song. It sounded like someone was squeezing a whole lot of accordions all at once. Quinn looked at her friends but then very quickly looked away so she didn't giggle.

"Wow. Your voices are so . . . unique!" she said.

"Thanks," said the Beat Badgers proudly. "Please, take the violin. And good luck!"

Carefully, Quinn picked up the instrument. She could feel its power surging through her paws. Somehow, she knew that the violin was happy to have been found.

She stroked the smooth wood as she put it in her magic bag. "You're safe with us, I promise," she murmured.

Quinn and her friends left the Beat Badgers to their dance party and flew deeper into the forest. They weaved through the tree trunks, swooping under fallen logs and over smaller shrubs.

"We've found the violin already!" Aisha called

in a singsong voice. "Should we take it straight back to the vault?"

Quinn shook her head as she swerved around an especially big tree trunk. "We need to find the strings and the bow first. If we return the violin like this, I have a feeling it won't have the same power."

"That sounds right," Mei called from behind, zigzagging her way closer to Quinn. "It's like a car without an engine. Maybe we can just replace those parts, though?"

Quinn scrunched up her snout. "I don't suppose there are any music shops around here!" she joked.

While they were flying, Quinn had the uncomfortable feeling that she was being watched. They were in a part of the forest where the trees grew densely. Not much sunlight made it through the trees, so it was hard to see and even harder to weave between the tall trunks. But every now and again, from the corner of her eye, Quinn thought she saw something move.

And now the buzzing, staticky sound she had heard when she first arrived was back. It was getting louder, too. "Be careful," she called softly to Mei and Aisha, who flew alongside her. "I think there might be Shadow Spr—!"

Before she could finish, a gray shape whooshed across her face and pulled the rest of her sentence right out of her mouth!

"Hey! Stop th—" she started to say, but once again, a Shadow Sprite darted over and tugged her words away.

Her heart began to pound, and it wasn't from

the flying. The Shadow Sprites were stealing her voice! She looked over at her friends to see if they had seen what happened. She could tell from their wide eyes that they had.

The Dragon Girls flew closer to one another, keeping up their speed and speaking in the faintest of whispers.

"If we stay quiet," Mei said, "then they can't steal our words."

Aisha made a face. "I guess so, at least until we figure out a way to beat them."

Quinn nodded as she tilted to one side to get through a narrow gap between two trees. She hated having her words snatched out of her mouth! It was better if she kept her words inside, where they were safe. She felt some-thing wispy and shadowy brush past her.

That's right, Dragon Girl. Just stay quiet. No one wants to hear you anyway!

Suddenly, Quinn stopped feeling scared. Now she just felt really, really mad! Sure, Quinn was the quietest of the Treasure Dragon Girls. And sure, she was shy to speak up or perform on her own in front of others. But when Quinn had something to say, it was important.

She deserved to be loud when she wanted to be! That was why she had chosen the trumpet as her instrument. It was her way of speak-ing up.

And in the Magic Forest, her roar was like

her built-in trumpet. She loved how it felt when she filled the air with the sound of roaring. She loved knowing that creatures for miles and miles could hear her. Roaring was her way of letting everyone know that although she was quiet, she could be really, really loud when it was important to be really, really loud. There was no way that she was going to let some awful Shadow Sprites silence her!

Quinn turned to her friends and mouthed, "On the count of three, let's roar our loudest roars."

Mei frowned and mouthed back, "Is that a good idea? Isn't that what the sprites want us to do, so they can steal our roars?"

"Maybe," Quinn mouthed. "But they are just puny shadows. We are dragons! If we all roar together, we'll blast them away."

Huge grins appeared on Mei's and Aisha's faces as they continued to speed through the forest. They were ready for action!

"One, two, three ..."

The Dragon Girls roared so loudly that the leaves on the trees blew back with the force. The group roar filled the air, and the sky lit up with streaks of ruby red, sapphire blue, and jade green. Caught up in the middle of the swirling colors were gray smears of shadow, tumbling over and over like lost socks in a whirlpool. The shadows got smaller and smaller until

they disappeared completely. Quinn felt like she could roar forever.

"That plan worked perfectly!" Mei said triumphantly as they came to a gentle stop in a clearing. She wrapped a wing around Quinn. "Those Shadow Sprites didn't stand a chance against our combined roar power."

"That's the thing about bullies, isn't it?" Aisha said, catching her breath after all that speedy flying and deep roaring. "They make you think there's no point trying to stand up to them. But when you do, you discover you're actually stronger than you knew. Especially when you team up with others!"

"Quinn, I have never heard you roar so loud!" Mei laughed. "My ears are still ringing."

Quinn chuckled. "Must be all my trumpet practice. Or maybe having the Heartstring Violin in my bag made me louder? It can't make any sound, so I have to make music for it."

"I can hear ringing, too," Aisha said, tilting

her head to one side. "But I don't think it's just in my ears."

"It's definitely not just in your ears!" said a voice nearby. "We've been trying to get your attention for a few minutes now!"

The Dragon Girls looked around curiously. All Quinn could see were spiderwebs, strung

between the branches of the trees and gleaming like silken threads. In the middle of one of the webs sat a little silver spider.

Quinn squinted. "Is that spider waving at us?" she asked her friends.

"Of course I'm waving at you!" called the spider. "I'm using four of my eight legs. You took your time noticing!"

"Sorry," said Quinn. "We're listening. Is there something you want to say?"

"No," said the spider. "But there is something you need to hear."

"Let me introduce myself. My name is Aria," said the silver spider.

Aria moved quickly over the threads of her web. As she touched each thread, there came a tinkling bell sound. It started low and went up a tone with each step until the notes were very high near the web's center.

Quinn felt a shiver of happiness. The notes were so clear and pure.

"Wow!" breathed Mei.

Aisha clapped her paws.

"That was just the warm-up," said Aria. "Now I'll play a real song."

Aria began to jump back and forth across her web, landing on one thread and then bouncing off to another. Each time she touched a thread, a beautiful clear note rang out.

It's like a harp crossed with the tinkling of a wind chime, thought Quinn, closing her eyes to fully enjoy the music. *But there's something else, too. It's the touch of magic!*

When the song finished, Aria took a deep

bow as the Dragon Girls clapped their paws furiously.

"Incredible!" Aisha said. "I didn't know spiderwebs could sound like that."

"Most can't," said Aria. "But I am a Song Weaver."

Something was bothering Quinn. "Why

haven't the Shadow Sprites stolen your sounds?" she asked.

"Oh, they keep trying," said Aria. "But my family and I have been spinning musical webs for as long as the Magic Forest has been here. They are no match for us. Also, we just bite them when they get close."

"You have family?" Quinn asking, trying to focus on that and not think about being bitten by a spider.

Aria put two of her feet to her mouth and gave a short, sharp whistle. From behind the leaves appeared hundreds of shiny silver spiders, some bigger and some smaller, their eyes all glittering like jewels.

Quinn heard Aisha gulp. "That's a big family," Aisha whispered. "I hope they aren't venomous."

"Of course we're venomous!" Aria replied. "We must protect ourselves."

"Exactly!" chorused the other spiders.

"Even before the Shadow Sprites gained strength, creatures were always trying to steal our music," Aria explained.

"Don't worry, we're not here to do that," said Quinn hastily. "We're in the middle of a quest right now."

"We know! We know!" said the spiders, rolling onto their backs and waving their legs in the air. "You have the Heartstring Violin."

"Our webs are very sensitive," Aria explained. "They catch hold of any sounds in the Magic Forest. Once they are caught, we can listen to them. We heard you talking with the Beat Badgers. We know you have the violin in your bag."

Quinn, Mei, and Aisha exchanged surprised looks. These spiders really did know everything.

"We're taking it back to the Magic Forest's treasure vault," Quinn said.

This seemed to upset the spiders, who began chattering. Their voices sounded like hundreds of little bells chiming at once.

"You can't return the violin yet!" they exclaimed. "It has no strings! If you take it back to the vault like that, the violin's magic won't work."

"We were worried that might be the case," admitted Mei. "Do you know where we could find violin strings?"

"You'll never find the violin's original strings," said Aria. "Once they've been removed, they turn to dust. That's so no one can put them on a new instrument. You see, there can only ever be one Heartstring Violin."

The Treasure Dragons looked at one another in dismay. What were they going to do?

A spider nearby began to play a sad-sounding tune on his web.

"That song fits how I'm feeling right now," Mei said.

"It *is* how you're feeling," said Aria. "Like I said, our webs are very sensitive. They pick up the feelings in the hearts of the creatures around them. That's why Song Weaver webs were used to make the strings of the Heartstring Violin."

Quinn stared at Aria, wondering if she'd heard correctly. "The strings were made from your webs?"

"Of course," said Aria. "What other web would they be made from?"

"Then you can make new ones!" Aisha said excitedly.

Aria tapped three of her feet to her face thoughtfully. "It's true. We could do that," she said. "But we'd need inspiration first. We can't just weave strings from nothing, you know. We can only weave important strings if we are listening to important music. Something that comes from the heart."

The Dragon Girls looked at one another. "I am not bad at whistling 'Happy Birthday,'" said Aisha. She began to whistle, but the spiders put all their legs over their heads in horror.

"No, no, NO! That won't do at all!" they cried.

Aria tiptoed across her web to be closer to the Dragon Girls.

"One of you has a special song inside you," she said. "I can hear it, faintly. It's beautiful. Can you let it out?"

"It's definitely not me." Mei laughed. "I am no singer!"

"As you just heard, it's not me, either," said Aisha.

Everyone looked over at Quinn, whose heart had begun to beat very fast. "I do have a song," she said nervously. "But it's very new. And I don't think I can play it without my trumpet."

"Try humming it," said Aria. "I have a feeling it will sound just as good that way."

"Go on, Quinn," urged Mei and Aisha.

Quinn *really* didn't want to sing in front of everyone. She hated solos! *But we must fix the violin*, she reminded herself. *It's okay to be a little embarrassed for something so important.*

Quinn closed her eyes, took a deep breath, and began to hum. The melody starting flowing from her. It was quiet to begin with, but

as she got more sure of herself, she hummed louder. There was more of the tune inside her than she'd realized! She got so caught up in it that she forgot to be self-conscious.

Quinn heard Aisha exclaim, "It's working!"

Quinn opened her eyes to see the Song Weaver spiders hard at work. They were speedily weaving four long, silvery strings!

She opened up the bag and carefully pulled out the Heartstring Violin.

"Cut the strings!" cried Aria.

Instantly, four spiders whipped out tiny, gleaming scissors and sliced the strings free. They floated into the air.

"No!" cried Mei. "They're flying away."

But Quinn could feel a vibration in the wood of the violin. "Don't worry," she said. "The violin is calling to the strings. Watch."

Sure enough, after looping through the air once, the strings began to settle down toward the violin. The vibrations in the violin grew steadily stronger as the four strings came to rest along the neck of the violin. They spread out in order, from thickest to thinnest. Deftly, they wrapped one of their ends around the pegs at the top of the violin and then stretched across the bridge of the instrument and attached themselves firmly to the other end.

The Heartstring Violin felt warm in Quinn's paws. A melody began to pour out of it. It was Quinn's tune!

The Song Weavers erupted into spidery cheers.

"It's fixed!" Aria said happily.

"Yes, thanks to you," said Quinn.

"We did it together," said Aria. "Which is how the best music is made."

Carefully, Quinn put the Heartstring Violin back in her bag. Now that it had strings, it felt even more powerful. A nearby spider jumped on its web, playing a happy tune that fit the Dragon Girls' mood perfectly.

"We've completed the quest!" Mei said.

"Not quite," Aria said. "You still need the bow."

"The bow?" repeated Aisha, wrinkling her snout. "We don't need to put a bow on the violin, do we? Surely all that matters is that we've found it."

Quinn shook her head. "Not a ribbon kind of bow. The kind of bow you use to play a violin."

Suddenly, she didn't feel quite so happy. Finding the bow might be difficult. The Song Weaver spiders huddled together, chattering softly.

Then Aria turned to the Dragon Girls. "We have heard through our webs that the bow is in the Realm of Birds," she said. "We suggest you try there."

"Thanks so much!" said Quinn. "How do we find it?"

"The Realm of Birds moves all the time," said Aria. "Normally it's easy to find. You simply follow the birdsong. But since the Shadow Sprites have been stealing the forest sounds, the birds have been very quiet. Your best chance is to ask a bird to lead you there."

Quinn smiled. "I know just the bird to help us. Flutterdash!" No sooner had she said the name than Quinn felt a presence at her side.

"Follow me!" said Flutterdash. Her voice was still weak, but her flying was as nimble as ever. She rose high into the air.

Quinn, Aisha, and Mei thanked the Song Weavers for their help, then flew off after Flutterdash. Once they were away from the spiders and their music, Quinn was struck once more by the unnatural silence of the Magic Forest. She could see the trees below her moving with the breeze, but she couldn't hear the leaves or the wind! A bee buzzed by her ear ... except there was no actual buzzing sound at all. Down below, the rivers made no sound as they flowed along. Even worse, the water didn't seem to know which way to go. It would flow in one direction for a bit. Then the waters would swirl around and go another way.

It's like when the band tries to play without a conductor, thought Quinn.

Then Quinn had a terrible thought. *What if the Magic Forest was silent forever?* Quinn shook the worry from her head. *We are NOT going to let that happen!* she promised herself.

Flutterdash flew up beside Quinn, coughed, and pointed down with her wing. Below them was a vast, colorful tapestry draped across the treetops. The tapestry was made of countless brightly colored birds! The birds were almost completely silent. All Quinn could hear was the occasional bird cough or low twittering.

Aisha and Mei were looking down, too. "That

must be the Realm of Birds down below, right?"
said Aisha.

Quinn nodded. "For sure. Let's go!"

Together, the three friends and Flutterdash
swooped toward the treetops, and then lower
until they touched down on the ground. Quinn
looked up with amazement. Upon every single
branch perched a bird. It was like being inside
a kaleidoscope filled with gemstones!

Quinn felt Mei nudge her. "What are they
doing?" she murmured, pointing to a group of
birds on a nearby branch.

It took Quinn a moment to work out what she
was seeing. Most of the birds looked perfectly

normal. But this little group had long and elaborate hairstyles. One had ringlets; another one had a high ponytail. One had a very elegant French twist while yet another had lots of tiny little pigtails here, there, and everywhere.

Quinn stifled a laugh. She didn't want to be rude, but the birds looked so funny!

"Are you laughing at us, Dragon Girl?" tweeted the bird with the high ponytail. She sounded huffy, but her voice was raspy and weak, as if she had a bad cold.

"I'm sorry," said Quinn, trying to keep a straight face. "I've never seen birds with such fantastic hairdos."

"We are the soloists," explained the bird with ringlets. "We lead the other birds in song. But when the Shadow Sprites took our voices, we needed to find another way to stand out. So we made ourselves wigs. The first wigs were made of grass, but they didn't last very long."

"Then we found something that worked much better," said the bird with the French twist, giving her 'do a proud pat with a wing.

"It looks like horsehair," Aisha whispered.

Quinn started. Violin bows were made from horsehair! Or at least, they were in the olden days. She turned to the birds. "Where did you find the hair for your beautiful wigs?"

"The hair was attached to that stick over there," said the bird with ringlets, pointing to something on the ground. Quinn pounced on it, her heart pounding. It was a violin bow. And it was made from the same kind of honey-colored wood as the Heartstring Violin! But a bow with no hair wasn't going to be of much use.

Quinn turned to face the soloist birds. "Are your wigs comfortable?"

"Not really," admitted the bird with the high ponytail.

"Not at all!" said the bird with the tiny pig-tails. "They are terribly itchy. But the other birds depend on us to lead the birdsong, which is very important in the Magic Forest. It tells the other creatures when to wake up. It warns them when danger is coming or food is nearby. And it lets others know when it's time for bed. Now that we don't have our voices to lead the group, we must rely on our wigs."

Quinn's mind whirred. She could see Aisha and Mei looking at her, hoping that she had an idea. She actually did have one, but she wasn't sure if it would work.

"Have you tried singing *together*?" she asked.

The birds looked at her in shock. "Like the name says, soloists sing alone," said the bird with ringlets.

"I know you usually do," said Quinn. "And when my friends and I have beaten the Shadow Sprites, you will again. But while your voices aren't at full strength, maybe you could try combining them?"

The birds shook their heads, causing their wigs to wobble. "Our voices are still so weak, and they're totally different. We can't even sing the same notes."

"That's okay. You could sing in harmony," said Quinn.

Before she could feel embarrassed, Quinn sang a low melody.

"Ooh, that's pretty!" said the bird with the ponytail, repeating it. Her voice was soft but had a beautiful tone.

"Perfect!" said Quinn.

Then she sang another melody, a little higher than the first. The bird with the ringlets copied her.

Quinn turned to the bird with the French twist. "This one is for you," she said, singing a tune that soared above the others.

The bird repeated it perfectly.

"Now, try all together," said Quinn, feeling a bit like the band leader.

The birds sang their parts. And although each of them was hard to hear when they sang alone, together they sounded much louder.

"Wow," exclaimed Mei, "that was so—"

Before she could finish her sentence, something very surprising happened. A wonderful sound rose up. The other birds had begun to sing! Their voices were weak, but when they all sang together, they still managed to fill the glade with music. Quinn got shivers listening to it.

Imagine how amazing they will sound once they get their full power back, she thought happily.

The soloists flew into the air. "Thank you, thank you, thank you!" they trilled softly, in perfect harmony. "Here, you can have these itchy wigs if you want them."

The birds shook their heads and the wigs tumbled down. Flutterdash darted out and caught each one neatly in her beak. She placed them in Quinn's paws.

It took Quinn a few moments to untangle the wigs. She was so excited that her paws were trembling. But the wonderful birdsong filling the air made it easier. Finally, she managed

to attach all the precious hairs back onto the bow.

"We've done it!" she cried, waving it in the air like a conductor.

With that, a new sound was added to the chorus of birds. The happy roars of Treasure Dragons!

Flutterdash landed on Quinn's shoulder.

"Someone needs to play the Heartstring Violin before it's returned to the vault," she tweeted softly. "We must get the forest back in tune."

"You play it, Quinn," said Aisha.

Mei nodded. "It has to be you."

"I'm a trumpet player," protested Quinn. "I don't know the first thing about playing the violin!"

"But you're musical," Aisha pointed out. "You've got a better chance of figuring it out than we do."

Quinn knew Aisha was right. And weirdly, she had the feeling the violin wanted her to play it. She picked it up. The wood felt warm. She reached for the bow and drew it across one of the strings.

A single, perfect note floated from the violin and hung in the air. Rather than getting fainter as the seconds passed, the note grew stronger and louder.

Quinn heard a faint rustling noise all around her. "Finally, I can hear the wind," she called to her friends.

Flutterdash rose into the air. "You must get the violin back to the vault as quickly as possible," she urged. "The Shadow Queen will not be happy. She might try to stop you. Hurry!"

As Flutterdash spoke, the sky darkened as if a storm was approaching. Quinn quickly tucked the violin and bow into her bag.

"Shadow Sprites!" yelled Mei.

"And they look angry," muttered Aisha.

Quinn looked up to see a mass of furious Shadow Sprites streaking toward them. The staticky noise was even louder now. The sound rattled through Quinn's head, making it hard to think.

"Let's roar them away!" Aisha said.

"Should we?" Quinn asked. Her head felt like it was full of cotton balls. She couldn't think clearly.

The Shadow Sprites began to dart toward the birds.

"They're trying to steal the birdsong." Mei groaned. "We have to do something!"

Mei and Aisha began to roar, and Quinn joined in. Soon the air filled with swirls of ruby red, sapphire blue, and jade green. The sight was glorious, right up until something terrible happened! A pack of Shadow Sprites grabbed the swirls and sucked them up like long strands of spaghetti.

"Stop roaring!" yelled Quinn to her friends.

But it was too late. Quinn watched as the Shadow Sprites pulled the roars directly from their mouths, like plants pulled up by the roots.

Furious, Quinn charged at the sprites with her head down, sending them flying in all directions.

"Mei? Aisha? Are you okay?" she cried, but only the tiniest whisper came out.

Her friends opened their mouths to speak, but they couldn't, either! The Shadow Sprites had not only stolen their roars, they'd stolen their voices!

Quinn's anger bubbled up inside her.

"Feeling angry, are you?" sneered a sinister voice. "You Dragon Girls thought that if you worked as a team, you could do anything. How wrong you were! You are no stronger together than you are alone."

Quinn whirled around. There, in the middle of the mass of Shadow Sprites, hovered a tall, thin woman in a billowing gray dress. Her long hair was gray, too. It was impossible to tell if she was old or young, but she was definitely mean. Her eyes gleamed nastily.

Quinn knew right away who this was: the

Shadow Queen. The urge to roar was very strong, but Quinn knew it would not help.

"Give us back our roars!" Quinn demanded. Her voice was weak, but she still sounded very determined.

"Never!" the Shadow Queen cackled.

And with that, she took off into the air, away from the Realm of Birds. The Shadow Sprites clustered around their queen, disappearing into the dark sky with her and the Dragon Girls' roars.

The Dragon Girls didn't need their voices to know what to do next. They flapped their wings and sped off after the roiling, twisting mass of shadows.

Soon they'd left the Realm of the Birds far behind. The Shadow Queen led them higher and higher into the mountains. The air grew icy, and yet somehow Quinn didn't feel cold. It was like a fire burned inside her.

We'll get them back, she told herself. *And we'll do it by working together.*

Hearing the birdsong and the wind had reminded Quinn how much she loved the sounds of the Magic Forest. She surged forward even faster.

It was odd to be flying in silence. Quinn was used to being the quietest in the group, but suddenly no one was speaking. Luckily, she knew her friends so well, they didn't need words. As she watched, a strange expression came over Aisha's face. Quinn followed her gaze and instantly knew what Aisha was thinking.

"We've been here before," Quinn said. "We're near the frozen lake with the dancing bears!"

It dawned on Quinn where they were going: the Shadow Queen's palace! Sure enough, a huge icy shape loomed through the fog. The palace's sharp towers seemed to pierce the air and a cold mist rose from its forbidding walls. Quinn shivered just looking at it. It did not look like a cozy place to live!

"We've got to stop the Shadow Queen before she locks your roars in the palace!" twittered Flutterdash.

Quinn already felt like she was flying at top speed, but she managed to find a little more energy. She surged forward again, getting so close to the Shadow Queen she could just about grab hold of her flowing gray dress.

But the Shadow Queen pulled away from Quinn's reach.

She laughed, waving the Dragon Girls' swirling roars in the air. "I am trapping your voices in my palace, and you'll never get them back! It won't be long until I have every sound in the Magic Forest. Then I'll take over from my sister as almighty ruler of the Magic Forest!"

Quinn froze. The Shadow Queen and the Tree Queen were sisters? She turned to her friends, seeing that they were as amazed as she was.

"Hard to believe, isn't it?" said the Shadow Queen, hovering in midair and narrowing her eyes. "My sister has always acted like she's better than me. But soon I'll be in charge. Everyone in the forest will do as I say."

Quinn did not like the sound of this at all. And neither did the Heartstring Violin! Quinn felt it shudder inside the bag. *It wants to get out!* thought Quinn. *But is that a good idea?*

Flutterdash whispered in her ear. "We don't have much time left! You must act!"

"But what should I do?" Quinn whispered in her raspy, weak voice.

"Just trust your feelings," twittered the bird.

The violin jumped around in the bag even more strongly. The Shadow Queen fixed her cruel, glittering eyes on Quinn as she pulled it out.

"I see you've stolen back the Heartstring Violin! Why don't you just return that to me?" purred the Shadow Queen. "If you do, I may even let you help me rule the Magic Forest. I could use a strong creature like you to keep everyone in line. Don't worry about your friends. They will just hold you back."

Mei's face darkened and Aisha looked like she was about to explode. Quinn shot them a reassuring look. As if she would leave them and help the Shadow Queen! But strangely, Quinn's arm wanted to hand the violin over, even though her head knew it was a bad idea. The Shadow Queen's magic was truly powerful.

Luckily, Aisha and Mei saw what was happening. They grabbed ahold of the violin, too, and dragged it back from the Shadow Queen. Quinn smiled gratefully at her friends. Then she held up the violin and positioned the bow above the strings.

Warmth spread from the honey-colored wood of the violin up Quinn's arm and throughout her entire body. The violin clearly liked the idea of being played again! The problem was that Quinn had no idea if she could actually play the violin. So far she'd made only a single note on it. She knew that much more was needed this time.

She glanced across at her friends, who were both smiling and nodding excitedly at her.

They think I can do it, Quinn thought. *So maybe I can!*

"Don't you dare try playing that violin, Dragon Girl!" yelled the Shadow Queen as the sprites twisted and tumbled around Quinn, tugging at her tail and wings and doing the same to Aisha and Mei. "You'll regret it!"

But Quinn paid her no attention. She closed her eyes and focused on the violin. Carefully, she pulled the bow across one of the shining silver strings. A note floated up, simple but clear. Then Quinn pressed down on two strings to form a chord. It was strange, but somehow she knew exactly what to do. Quinn felt like she was being guided by the violin.

Quinn continued to play, teasing out one note and gliding into the next. The more she played, the more confident she became. A strange and beautiful song began to flow from the violin. The music sounded like the wind in the trees. Like babbling water flowing over smooth stones. Like insects humming and bunnies playing. Like a mother bird returning to her nest to feed her chicks.

It's music from the heart of the Magic Forest, Quinn realized.

"Stop playing that horrible racket!" bellowed the Shadow Queen. She looked angry, but Quinn saw something else in her eyes, too. She was worried!

A strong wind picked up around the Shadow Queen, blowing her long hair into messy tangles. She lunged at Quinn with her impossibly long, thin fingers. Quinn darted away, but the Shadow Queen managed to grab ahold of the compass dangling around her neck. With an angry shout, the queen broke the compass chain and flung the precious object into the air.

With a slow, perfect arc, the compass dropped into the lake far below them.

Quinn wanted to shout in dismay, but without her voice, all she could do was keep playing the violin. So that's what she did. And finally something wonderful happened: The red and blue and green roars that the Shadow Queen had stolen broke free of her shadowy clutches!

"Come back!" shrieked the Shadow Queen, lunging at the colorful roars.

But the roars blew up out of her reach, like ribbons in a storm. They circled through the

air before floating down toward Mei, Aisha, and Quinn. The moment they made contact with their owners, the colors disappeared.

"I've got my voice back!" yelled Aisha, doing a midair loop of joy.

"Me too!" Mei cried. "Keep playing, Quinn!"

Quinn kept playing, and the music filled the cold air with warmth. The annoying buzzing sound of the Shadow Sprites was soon drowned out by the beautiful melody. While Quinn played, Mei and Aisha roared their bright, powerful roars. The colors seeped into the murky grays of the queen and her sprites.

For a terrible moment, the gray nearly swallowed the ruby reds and sapphire blues. But then Mei and Aisha roared at the top of their voices. With a sound like water being poured on hot coals, a huge cloud of gray simply disappeared. The remaining shadows were flung out in all directions.

Then there was another sound: a loud cracking one.

"Wow. Look!" cried Aisha. She pointed a talon at the Shadow Queen's palace.

A turret crumbled into tiny shards of ice, followed by another, and another. The palace was falling apart! As more of the palace cracked and tumbled, a river of melted ice began flowing down the mountain.

"You rotten Dragon Girls!" the Shadow Queen shrieked. "You're destroying my palace!"

"Yes! We did it!" said Quinn, grinning at her friends.

In a fury, the Shadow Queen whipped away from Quinn and her friends and dove headlong into the strange mist hovering about the palace.

Yet another section of the palace crumbled into icy shards and the Dragon Girls could hear the Shadow Queen raging at her sprites. "Make this stop!" she yelled. But there was nothing the sprites could do.

"What is *that*?" Mei asked suddenly.

Quinn stopped playing and looked. A mist rose up from the crumbling remains of the castle. Unlike normal mist, this one was making a sound. But not just one sound. The mist was filled with hundreds of different sounds! There were squawks and barks and the sound of a waterfall. There were frogs and insects and the rustling of leaves.

"It's the stolen sounds of the Magic Forest!" Quinn gasped.

The melodious mist rose from the crumbling palace. It hung in the air for a moment, then scattered in all directions

"After them, sprites!" the Shadow Queen commanded.

"No way!" Mei growled. "Come on, Dragon Girls."

Quinn grinned as she and her fierce friends

chased the remaining Shadow Sprites, roaring at them to protect the escaping sounds. The palace was melting very rapidly now. A huge body of water had formed and was tumbling down the mountainside, gaining force with every second.

Finally, with a loud crash, the central tower of the palace imploded, sending water and ice crystals showering into the air.

"We did it!" cried Aisha as the wails of the Shadow Queen were drowned out by sheets of crushing ice.

"Watch out!" yelled Quinn, tucking the Heartstring Violin and bow back into her bag and speeding over to her friends.

Two massive waves reared up from where the palace had been. The first wave crashed over the Shadow Queen and the remaining sprites, picking them up and carrying them off. As the wave tumbled, it flattened the remains of the palace, smoothing it away to nothing.

The second wave zoomed toward Quinn and her friends, lifting them up on its crest and carrying them along.

The wave was very powerful, but Quinn wasn't afraid. She had a feeling this wave was going to help them. Without the compass, Quinn didn't know how they would find the vault. But one thing was for sure: It would be quicker to ride the wave down the mountain than to fly!

"Do either of you know how to surf?" Quinn called across to Mei and Aisha.

"No," they yelled back.

"Me neither." Quinn laughed. "But I think we're about to learn!"

As the water rose up beneath Quinn, she stretched out her wings for balance. Mei and Aisha did the same.

"Hey, this is fun!" Mei exclaimed.

"Do you think we're the first ever dragons to learn how to surf?" Aisha called back.

"Definitely!" said Quinn.

The huge wave of water sped down the mountain as fast as a bullet train. Quinn felt the wind rushing past as she and her friends surfed the wave. Even better, she could hear more and more of the forest sounds returning.

There was another sound, too: the heartbeat of the Magic Forest that Quinn had heard when they first set out. "It's stronger now," she mused. "And more steady."

Flutterdash, who was riding along on Quinn's shoulder, leaned forward. "The strong forest heartbeat is thanks to you three," she chirped. "You overpowered the Shadow Queen!"

Quinn felt a warm glow. The feeling was similar to how she felt when the band perfected a song. It was so special to create something with others. As Quinn zoomed along the rap-ids with her friends, Quinn thought about how it felt to play the Heartstring Violin while everyone listened. She never thought she'd be able to do that!

But, in fact, she had enjoyed it. *Maybe doing a solo isn't too scary after all*, she thought.

"Look, there's Stone Face!" Aisha yelled suddenly.

Quinn looked up. She'd been so deep in thought, she hadn't noticed how far they'd traveled. But Aisha was right. Up ahead was the carved stone face that guarded the entrance to the vault. The wave of water had now become part of the mighty river that flowed through the forest. Cheering animals gathered along the banks of the river, waving at the Dragon Girls as they passed by. It was like surfing through a parade!

When the river flowed by the entrance to the vault, Quinn, Aisha, and Mei jumped off the wave and pulled themselves up the riverbank.

"Welcome, Treasure Dragon Girls!" Stone Face called. His smile stretched so wide that Quinn was worried he might crack. "I know you've found the Heartstring Violin because the forest is full of sound again. The soldier ants have been singing nonstop for an hour now!"

"Yes, we have it," Quinn said, shaking herself dry and patting the bag with the violin and bow. "Can you open the vault so we can put it back where it belongs?"

"Of course," said Stone Face. "Right after you say a few words. I like to make opening the door a special occasion."

Once, Quinn would've felt too shy to say anything. But the quest had changed her, and she knew exactly what to say.

"Music is life itself," she called out.

"It certainly is!" Stoney's smile stretched even wider.

With a rumbling sound, the heavy door of the vault slid open. It didn't matter how many times Quinn stepped inside the vault; it was always thrilling. The Treasure Dragons flew down the entrance tunnel, lit with its multi-colored lights, until they reached the main cavern. This huge space glowed with a golden light. Diamond necklaces dripped like stalac-tites from the roof, and shiny coins covered

the floor. Everywhere Quinn looked, something twinkled brightly. Quinn felt joy bubbling inside her. She loved being in here, surrounded by beautiful things.

Quinn had a job to do, though, so she tried to focus. In the middle of the cavern stood three columns. On the first was the Forest Book, which they had rescued on their first quest. On the second was the Magic Mirror, which they had returned on their last visit.

One column remained empty. Quinn walked toward it, feeling the Heartstring Violin vibrate as she got closer. "Almost home," she whispered to the instrument.

Quinn undid the bag and pulled out the violin and bow. The violin began to hum, and the happy sound filled the cavern. Quinn placed the violin and bow gently on the column. She felt a little sad to leave it. She had grown fond of it.

"Listen to this," said Mei, opening the Forest Book to the most recent page.

Quinn felt a little sad to leave the violin. She

had grown fond of it. And the violin had grown fond of her! But it made a silent promise to Quinn: Every time she played music, the Heartstring Violin would add just a little bit of magic.

Smiling, Quinn gave the Heartstring Violin one last stroke, feeling the warmth of its honey-colored wood seep into her. "I'll think of you whenever I play music," she said.

Just then, Flutterdash flew over. "It's time to get going," she trilled, her voice rich and strong now that the Shadow Queen's palace had melted. "The Tree Queen wishes to see you all."

The Treasure Dragons gazed around the vault one final time before flying back along the tunnel and to the outside.

"Goodbye, Stoney!" Quinn called to the beaming stone face as she and her friends rose high into the clear blue sky.

"Farewell, Treasure Dragons!" Stone Face said in his gravelly voice. "Come back anytime for a sing-along with me and the soldier ants."

"We will, for sure!" Quinn laughed.

Together, the three friends flew high over

the treetops toward the glade. Every bird in the forest seemed to be singing. Quinn and the others twirled and looped to the forest music as they traveled along. It was like having a midair dance party.

Soon, down below, Quinn spotted the shimmering force field around the glade. Flutterdash flew up to Quinn and gave her a gentle peck goodbye.

"It was fun going on this quest with you," she twittered. "And thank you for returning my voice. Come back soon!"

"I will," Quinn promised.

They stepped through the warm shimmery air of the force field. Inside the glade, the Tree

Queen waited for them. Her branches were filled with tiny brightly colored birds, singing with all their might.

"Congratulations, Treasure Dragons!" said the Tree Queen warmly. "You have returned the melodies of my forest and severely weakened the Shadow Queen's power."

"So she still has some powers?" Mei asked.

The Tree Queen nodded her wise head. "It's almost impossible to destroy a shadow. And anyway, we need shadows. Just as we need both night and day, summer and winter. The trick is to stop her from gaining too much power and using it for evil."

"You have one mean sister," muttered Aisha.

The Tree Queen smiled gently at that and said simply, "I will always be grateful for your help."

"We were happy to help!" Mei said.

"Absolutely," agreed Aisha. But Quinn didn't reply. She had suddenly remembered something she needed to tell the Tree Queen.

"I lost the compass," she admitted. "It fell into the lake near the Shadow Queen's palace." The Tree Queen nodded. "Yes. My birds told me. But don't worry; it will find its way back to me. It always does. It takes more than a little water to destroy such a powerful instrument."

Quinn smiled in relief. Suddenly, she felt so much lighter!

"It is now time for you to return home, my Treasure Dragons," said the Tree Queen. "But first, I have a gift for each of you."

She shook a branch and three little charms fell onto the soft mossy grass next to their friendship bracelets. Each one was shaped like a tiny golden coin, with the outline of a leaf etched into it.

"You can add these to your friendship bracelets," said the Tree Queen, "so you remember that the Magic Forest is also a friend."

Quinn picked up her bracelet and new charm and held them in her paws. They would always remind her of her Magic Forest adventures.

"See you at jewelry class next week?" Mei asked, wrapping her wings first around Quinn and then around Aisha.

Quinn felt her heart beating extra fast as she made a quick decision. "My school band has a concert tomorrow, and I'm playing a solo. Would you like to come?"

"Are you kidding?" Aisha grinned.

"Try to stop us!" Mei said.

As Quinn watched the jade-green light growing out of her bracelet, she felt warm and happy. It was sad to leave the Magic Forest.

But it was exciting to think she would see her friends tomorrow!

Through the green swirl of color, Quinn could see the faint outline of the band room. She stepped into the green light and felt herself being pulled back into the real world.

"Goodbye for now, Magic Forest!" she murmured as her feet lifted off the ground and she spun around and around. "I hope to see you again one day!"

❧

Quinn sat onstage, her trumpet on her lap. All around her, the other band members were getting ready for the performance. Quinn was wearing her good black pants and a freshly ironed white

shirt. Her friendship bracelet was tucked under her shirtsleeve. She couldn't see the coin charm the Tree Queen had given her, but just knowing it was there made her feel stronger.

She looked out at the audience. The chairs were filling up! And there, in the front row, sat Mei and Aisha. They waved excitedly at her. She grinned and waved back.

Just then, Ms. Tran approached. "How are you feeling, Quinn?" she asked.

"Nervous about doing a solo," she admitted, "but I am doing it anyway."

"I am so happy to hear that," Ms. Tran said.

Quinn's nerves fluttered in her stomach until the moment she began playing. Then, like magic, her nerves disappeared. The melody filled her up, leaving no room for worry.

And as she played, Quinn felt the magic in every note. When she finished, the audience broke into applause. Aisha and Mei clapped the hardest of all!

ABOUT THE AUTHORS

Maddy Mara is the pen name of Australian creative duo Hilary Rogers and Meredith Badger. Hilary and Meredith have been collaborating on books for children for nearly two decades.

Hilary is an author and former publishing director, who has created several series that have sold into the millions. Meredith is the author of countless books for kids and young adults, and also teaches English as a foreign language to children.

The Dragon Girls is their first time co-writing under the name Maddy Mara, the melding of their respective daughters' names.

Oh my glaciers, Diary!

Princess Lina is the *coolest* girl in school!

 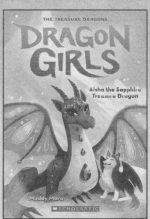